A *Steve Parish* **KIDS** Story Book

Frilled Friend

Story by Rebecca Johnson

Photos by Steve Parish

A very ordinary brown lizard stretched out in the afternoon sun.

There was nothing special about him. He wasn't covered with beautiful patterns and interesting colours as some lizards are.

To make it worse, he had loose and saggy skin around his neck. It made him look quite odd.

He kept to himself most days,
quietly lying in the sun,
waiting for insects
to come his way.

Just before sunset, the Spinifex Hopping-mice came out of their burrows and saw the odd looking lizard.

They had never seen such a lizard with so much skin around its neck.

Day after day, the lizard
sat quietly on his favourite branch.

The mice raced from place to place chatting about the strange lizard...

But as time went on, they paid less and less attention to it.

One evening, the mice were scurrying about looking for food.

The birds in the trees became strangely quiet. The tiny mice stopped and looked around but they could see nothing.

Then, with a rustle and crash, a huge monitor entered the clearing!

He saw the frightened mice and charged towards them.

They all took off, leaping and hopping, trying to outrun the enormous Sand Monitor!

The monitor was much bigger than they were and was very quick. He was gaining on them fast.

The little mice rushed for the cover of the grasses. They were almost there...

Suddenly something appeared in front
of the mice,
hissing loudly.

It had a huge frill around its neck and a wide yellow mouth. They froze with fear.

The strange creature
hurtled forward,
but did not stop
when it reached
them. It ran
straight past,
charging
towards
the monitor.

The monitor was terrified. He had never seen anything like it.

He turned around and quickly ran away.

The strange creature kept chasing after him,
hissing and showing its sharp teeth.

From behind a log, the hopping-mice realised it was the strange lizard they often ignored.

The loose, saggy skin had turned into a large frill and made him look ferocious.

When the Frilled Lizard returned
the mice were very grateful.

"We didn't know
you could do that!"
they cried.

"Ah," smiled the Frilled Lizard, "things are not always as they seem. My frill may look a little odd but it comes in very handy sometimes."